Whistle Like a Bird

Written by Sarah Vazquez
Illustrated by Francisco Mora

STECK-VAUGHN
COMPANY
ELEMENTARY • SECONDARY • ADULT • LIBRARY

I want to whistle like a bird.

Grandma shows me how to whistle like a bird.

I want to howl like a dog.

Grandma shows me how to howl like a dog.

I want to sing like a star.

Grandma shows me how to sing like a star.

Together we make a concert.